THE FONTEV...

BY TERESA DOLAN

With illustrations by Jean McCree

Chapter 1

William Arrives in Fontevraud l'abbaye.

"Out of the way William!" shouted Mother as she came barging through the front door of their new home balancing a pile of boxes on her outstretched hands like a circus performer. She practically fell over poor William, who looked up at her full of dismay and confusion at his new surroundings in this new village in a new country.

"Is this what you've brought me to?" meowed William "Absolute chaos! I didn't want to move to France in the first place, and secondly that man over there has just trodden on my tail!", William hissed and spat.

"Goodness William", said Mother, "pull yourself together. It's not the first time we've moved and I dare say it won't be the last. We'll have to put *you* in the attic!"

Mother did not understand how William was feeling. "Pull myself together", meowed William, "How on earth am I supposed to do that?". Of course Mother just wanted to get through the door with some more boxes, but William was confused. Father followed along with a troupe of men who were unloading a large white van which was stationed in the street with the words

"Man with a van" emblazoned on its side. Mother and Father were unloading the car.

"Come on Wills, let's take you upstairs", said Father sympathetically as he lifted William up into his arms and carried him to the attic. William purred as Father kissed his fur. He then shut the door leaving William to spin round and see where he was.

William was a large, agile tabby cat with twinkling yellow eyes and the sweetest of faces. His whiskers were white and long and his fur had stripy, jet black markings all over it. His tummy was extremely fluffy. He decided that the only thing to do on this particular occasion was to have a good wash, then stretch out, have a lovely yawn and go to sleep and pretend that all this "moving into a new home business", not to mention to a new country – France of all places – wasn't actually happening! He missed England. He had lived there since he was a kitten. It seemed strange to now be in this new country of France, where the air was heavily scented with unusual new scents and smells, such as hot chocolate, coffee and garlic; and where everyone spoke a different language.

He began to dream about being a kitten again and drifted off into the deepest of sleeps imagining that he was tucked up in Mother and Father's bed.

No sooner had he nodded off then the next thing that he knew there was a tap on his shoulder and a pesky looking mouse was eye-balling him and making strange sounds that he couldn't understand. It sounded to William like "oo la la oo la la" and not the usual "squeak, squeak, squeak" that he was used to hearing back in the south-east of England in Tunbridge Wells in Kent.

The mouse was wearing a little black hat on the side of his head and he began to tickle William's whiskers, giggling as he did so.

"Don't you dare", William tried to swipe the mouse with his paw, but the mouse ran away screeching with laughter and disappeared into a tiny hole into the rafters of the attic. William liked nothing better than to chase mice, but this mouse was especially fast and he just couldn't catch him.

That was the first encounter he had with a French mouse, and it soon followed that it was not to be his last.

Chapter 2

William was sitting on his front doorstep and looking around at the stone walls and stony paths and feeling lost.

It was a week since he and his family had moved into this new house in Fontevraud l'abbaye in France and he still wanted to go home to England. He hated this new house with the stairs and the strange rooms and neighbours who spoke only French.

He wanted to be back in the safe, little house in the South-East of England in Tunbridge Wells in the County of Kent. Here he had left behind all his friends, and a few enemies. He certainly would not be missing that big, fluffy cat, Bernard, who was always trying to stop him from climbing over the fence to the right of the house. A picture of Bernard suddenly came into William's mind and he began to think that in fact he rather missed him with his large, fluffy face and big green eyes.

William also missed the garden where he could climb trees and play with the dragonflies. He especially enjoyed the smell of freshly mown grass and the scent of spring flowers first thing in the morning when the dew was still on them and he could lick the water off of the petals and quench his thirst. His particular favourites being the large wild daisy's and buttercups which during the heat of the summer months flourished at the back of his garden where he would hide and play.

The meadow at the back of hi garden where William used to play when he lived in England

In the busy neighbourhood of his home town in England he could spy on passing neighbours including people, birds and mice going about their day-to-day business.

But, now his family had moved to this enormous house with no garden in the Loire Valley, which was supposedly called "The Garden of France" though he could see no evidence of a garden in this stony street.

He knew nobody, except that is for the horrible mice who lived in the walls of the house and kept popping up at the most inappropriate times such as when he was tucking into a fish supper, or trying to have a nice snooze. They knew his name now and were constantly calling "William! William!" in very high-pitched voices from inside the walls, so that he could not get to them.

"Blast, blast them, blast them", William moaned twitching his tail as he did so as he always did when he was cross.

If they were not trying to steal his food they would be trying to wake him up with lots of noise. For some reason Mother and Father never seemed to hear them. It made him feel sick.

He would have gone outside to get away from them, but he was too scared to even put a paw out of the front door.

As the days went by, William began to feel more confident and brave. Each morning he would sit on the front door step and watch the children walk past on their way to school.

Some of them even smiled at him and waved, though he could not understand a word that they said as they were speaking French and he only understood English. William thought, "I really must learn how to Meow in French".

One day a little girl called Melody with bright yellow hair stroked him and gave him a big kiss. William purred and loved every moment, but as soon as she had stopped to pat him, her Mother called out.

William could only imagine what she was saying, but he thought that it was probably something like "Melody, leave that cat alone or we shall be late for school".

Oh dear, thought William I wish *I* could go to school. Why doesn't someone invent a cat school, then I could learn how to meow in French and I would understand what the children are saying when they pass by each morning.

Still, William reflected that at least the children seemed to like him and their friendly faces lifted his spirits and made him feel a little happier.

Leaving the house itself was an altogether, different matter and he was still too scared to do this. Instead William just watched and waited for the right moment to venture out into the street.

Fontevraud is a pretty, village, and William's house is next to the famous Abbey where English Kings such as Henry II is buried, and French Queens, such as his wife Eleanor of Aquitaine have lived and who William was sure must have had cats of their own.

He wondered if those cats from the past still walked about the abbey, as he had often seen the ghosts of cats walking around Tunbridge Wells usually dressed in the most peculiar clothes such as wigs on their heads and fancy waistcoats. William had thought them terribly pretentious.

If William tilted his head to the left he could see lots of grown-up people, and children, going in, and coming out, of the abbey.

William longed to visit this place himself as he was sure that there would be a garden there, cats to play with and perhaps talk to (if that is he learnt French or they spoke English) and even "oh joy" mice and birds he could actually chase instead of being tormented by at home.

In England William had loved to chase birds and mice, he never hurt them he just liked to tease them.

On the other hand his views on mice were changing and he thought that if only he could catch the ones in his new house his life would be vastly improved.

One day when he was feeling particularly adventurous. He stepped out on to the street and no sooner had he reached the middle of the road, then a gigantic camper van came thundering down the street and nearly knocked poor William over. He shot back through his front door under the skirts of his Mother.

She was of course a human being, but she and her husband had looked after and loved him since he was five weeks old and he felt safe under Mother's long, sweeping skirts. William vowed never to go out again lest he be killed.

Chapter 3

A new day dawned, and instead of not going outside William decided to try again. He looked carefully down the street before he nervously stepped from his doorstep. His little face looked from the left, and to the right side of the road, and he listened and saw and heard that it was clear for him to make his crossing. He found a lovely sunny doorstep and after sniffing it, decided to take a sun-bathe and roll about on the dusty step.

This was bliss and it was almost as good as his birthday, when each year his human Mother and Father treated him to extra cuddles and a plate of smoked salmon.

William began to snooze away the day. He tried to keep one eye open in case something interesting was going on over the road at his home, but he felt so comfortable that he fell into a deep, deep sleep.

"Hey you, Monsieur…what do you think you are doing on *my* doorstep".

William woke up with startled eyes and was just about to dart back across the road to his home, when he decided that he rather liked the look of this cat who was actually speaking to him in English. He was a slinky and sleek black cat with bright blue eyes and a husky, French accent. And as William had no new friends, certainly not from the French cat-world, he decided to answer him.

"Hello", William nervously told him his name and pointed his paw across the road.

"That's my house opposite, across the street. "I've been living there for three whole weeks". William went on to explain that this was the first time that he had ventured outside.

"How did you know to meow to me in English?", William asked.

"My dear friend, I knew because I've heard you meowing from inside your house. Are you English, or are you an American?" asked the cat.

Monsieur Louis, a sleek black cat with the
brightest of blue eyes.

"I am English, said William, "and I'm afraid my French meowing is not very good".

"No Monsieur Anglais, it is *not*, but perhaps I can help you. My name is Monsieur Louis and I would be happy to teach you how to meow in French".

Now Monsieur Louis was a slinky and sleek black cat with bright blue eyes and William was thrilled that this rather confident cat wanted to be his friend and was happy to teach him how to meow in French. William felt very lucky to have met him.

"Thank you", said William. "That would be such a help". He told Louis about Melody, and how he wished that he understood her and the other children.

"Oh children", said Louis, "I suppose they are all right. Quite frankly though I get a bit tired of them trying to stroke me all the time. Sometimes they even pull my tail which of course leads to tears because as soon as they do that I bite them".

"Bite them!" William was shocked, but still he liked Louis and wanted to be his friend. He also thought that if some of the children pulled his tail that was *not* a very nice thing to do.

"If I was going to bite anyone", said William "It would be those pesky mice that live in my house".

"Pesky mice?", asked Louis and William told him how from dawn until dusk the mice were out to get him!

"Then", said Louis "I think we should teach them a lesson".

"How can we do it Louis?"

Louis had to think a bit and then he said "Quite simply my new found friend, we will set a trap!"

"A mouse trap?" questioned William "Nothing too cruel I trust, even though they deserve it", said William. William was a gentle cat and although he did get quite cross from time to time, he hated violence of most kinds and idea of a setting a mouse trap filled him with horror.

"Set your mind at rest mon petit", Louis reassured William "We will get them to disgrace themselves. It will take time and planning, but we will do it!"

It was nearly Christmas time and the parents had bought some brandy liqueurs and special chocolates over with them from England and had put them away in a chest in the attic. That evening they had gone to a party leaving William on his own in the house.

Louis suggested that they have there own party and so they opened the chest where the brandy liqueurs and chocolates that had been put away for Christmas and set them out on the table at the centre of the attic.

"Now we will simply leave and I wonder what will happen", Louis winked at William.

"But the mice, the mice – they will eat the chocolates and might well try to drink the liqueur", William called out in alarm.

"Maybe they will, and maybe they won't", said Louis and he winked at William.

Louis left for home and William went downstairs and fell asleep in Mother and Father's Bedroom. The next thing William knew it was early next morning and Mother and Father were shouting. William came running to see what all the commotion was about only to discover that both the chocolate and the liqueurs had been utterly consumed by the mice who it rather looked had had a party of sorts.

All of the music was over the floor and the piano lid was open. Chocolate wrappers were strewn everywhere and it was clear from the mess that the pesky mice had had a very good time.

Of course Mother and Father hadn't a clue who had done this "dreadful thing" and called the local Police (who in France are incidentally called the Gendarmes) and lodged a complaint that they had been burgled though in fact nothing appeared to have been stolen apart that is from

"All our Christmas chocolates and our Brandy Liqueur!",
exclaimed a very perplexed Mother.

"It is probably mice", the Gendarme advised them.
To this day, Mother and Father have no definite idea
who had held the party. Suffice it to say that although
Mother and Father could hardly believe that mice were
responsible for such chaos they sealed up all the mouse
holes in the house just in case. This pleased William very
much and the mice never bothered him again. At least
not in his own home.

A Pesky mouse

Chapter 4

William asked Louis how long he had lived in Fontevraud.

"My family and I have lived in this village for hundreds of years".

"Hundreds of years" said William. "How is this possible?"

"Well" said Louis, "you probably will not believe me unless I show you, but this is a really ancient place, and if you focus hard enough you can see, and be friends with not only cats from the past, but also cats from the future".

William thought about this for a moment. Of course he had seen spirit cats before, but had never been able to talk to them, let alone be friends with them.

"Goodness", said William could you really show me how to meet these cats? It is just that I have been quite lonely, as all my friends are in England and although I love my human parents it is lonely being an only cat in a strange country.

Louis thought for a moment, and then said, "Can you keep a secret?"

"Yes of course" breathed William.

"You must promise not to tell any humans, not even your parents." William nodded and crossed his paws.

"Then I will take you through the time tunnel where we will have lots of adventures together. You will meet cats, from the past, and also from the future. Children, too"

William was full of gratitude at the kindness of this stranger who was rapidly becoming his new best friend.

"I will happily teach you how to learn to meow in French, and we will also go on some adventures together".

William was thrilled about all of these new possibilities and was so happy he could hardly keep still.

"Oh Monsieur Louis I would love to come with you. How does it work? How can we travel back to the past, and be in the present and visit the future? Will it take long? Does it take longer if we go back to the past, or if we have a day out in the present, or if we go to the future? Should I have my lunch first? I'd really like to visit the abbey".

William was getting more and more excited and was speaking so quickly that Louis had to calm him down.

"William, although I can meow and understand some English, please speak slowly or we will misunderstand each other and then we will get confused and will not know what we are doing and that might lead to us getting cross with each other and falling out!"

William promised to speak slowly.

"Oh please Monsieur Louis when will we travel? Can we go now?"

Louis suggested that this would be all too much for the first time that a cat has been out onto a new street and that William should go home, have his lunch and then have a nice, long, snooze and come out again when it was night time.

"Before I go, could you please tell me what and where the time tunnel is or I shall never be able to sleep."

"The time tunnels are down the drains of Fontevraud", Louis explained, "and sometimes they occur in other places; sometimes quite unexpected places such as mirrors and pictures.

"Sounds as if we could get very dirty if we have to go down the drains".

"Not at all William". The drains of Fontevraud are filled with magic and they protect us from all sorts of things including dirt".

William breathed a sigh of relief as he liked to keep his coat glossy and in peak condition.

"Where shall I meet you, and at what time?" said William.

"When St. Michael's clock strikes midnight is the time, and the place we shall meet is on your doorstep".

"Goodbye Louis, see you later" said William. "I am *so* excited and am really looking forward to our adventures".

"It really is no good Monsieur if you are too excited, because if you are you create too much energy and then it is not possible to travel anywhere let alone back to the past, and you might as well forget about visiting the future altogether".
William returned home and ate a nice big lunch, and was so thirsty that he drank two large dishes of water.

"Goodness William," said his Mother, "you are thirsty and hungry today". William purred richly and rubbed himself against Mother's leg, then ran up the stairs as fast as his little legs could carry him and fell asleep in his cat basket for many hours.

Chapter 5

William woke up to the sound of a very loud bang.

"Meow, what is that?"

Mother and Father were nowhere to be seen and William was a little worried.

"Oh dear, where are they?"

William looked all over the house and saw that on each of the four landing floors dishes of cat food was piled high along with extra dishes of clean water.

There was also a note on the Dining-Room Table which read:

"Dearest William, we are terribly sorry, but we've unexpectedly had to go away for a couple of days. We have left the side window ajar for you, but as we know that you don't really like going out anymore you might prefer to keep it shut. We have also left you lots to drink and eat so you won't go hungry. Lot's of love....missing you already. Mother and Father".

"Oh no, how dreadful, how could they leave me all alone in this weird house, in this strange country and just when I was beginning to think that things might be improving!".

William suddenly felt very alone again and a little frightened. He was also concerned about the big bang that he had heard. He trooped down to the ground floor and peered through the glass pane of the front door.

The glass was decorated with little gold images of flowers which Mother said the French call "Fleurs de Lys", but that looked like the irises that grew round the pond at the back of his old house where he used to chase frogs.

Pressed against the glass this time was not just images of flowers, but also the gigantic flat face of a black cat looking very peculiar. William nearly jumped out of his fur, until he realised that it was not a gigantic cat face at all, but rather Louis's face magnified on the glass with a not altogether happy expression on it.

Louis for about the fifteenth time, banged on the door and glared through the glass, but this time he was shouting

"Monsieur William, it is very rude not to keep a rendezvous and ours was scheduled for ten minutes ago!"

William leapt up to the door handle and tried to open the door, but it could not open as there was no key in the lock. He called out that he was "very sorry".

He explained that he had been in a deep sleep, and simply had not realised the time.

"Normally my parents would have been making noises and picking me up and stroking me, but instead they have had to go away. Louis I am so sorry, but I am now *really* alone in France".

William could feel the tears welling up in his eyes. For one thing he could not get outside, and for another he could not even let his new friend in. Then he suddenly remembered that his parents had left the side window ajar and so it was that Louis first visited William's house.

Monsieur Louis, sleek and slim...

Chapter 6

No sooner did Louis come through the window then he playfully swiped William with his paw as he could see just how upset William was.

"My dear new friend do cheer up. It's not *so* bad, I will look after you and surely your parents are returning?"

"Oh yes", said William, but it was all such a shock waking up to a big bang and finding them gone".

Louis apologised for banging so loudly on the door and explained that it was a jolly good thing that he had or William might not have awoken until tomorrow and they had some important business to attend to.

"I'm sorry", said William "but I would really like to attend to some important business, I really would".

"Well firstly" said Louis, "I would like to have a dish of your famous English tea and then we shall go on our first adventure. By the way, do you have any English sweets?"

William showed Louis the cupboard where all the good things to eat were kept and whilst he made them both a dish of tea, Louis began to eat some English sweets and biscuits. William asked a little nervously that Louis not make a mess and be careful what he ate.

He certainly did not want a repetition of the Mice Party and the effect that this had had on his Mother and Father.

Louis seemed to be enjoying himself very much until he opened a jar and put his paw in it thinking that it would be another tasty thing that he could eat. Next William knew Louis was pulling the most awful face and looking at his paw, which was covered with a thick, slick of black goo. Louis screamed out in French

"Ugh, c'est terrible"

and then in English

"Ugh, this is horrible".

William wondered what on earth was the matter until he discovered that in fact Louis had opened a jar of English Marmite which as anyone who has ever tried Marmite will know is either the most delicious of things to eat, or is indeed the most revolting of foods.

William explained that whether you like to eat Marmite or not, it is not meant to be eaten like that.

"My parents have it on toast, but in my experience cats rarely eat it and are silly to even try".

"Touché", said Louis. "Now we are equal. I've managed to frighten you, and you've managed to tell me off and all in the space of half an hour!"

Next the two friends turned off the lights, sprung up to the window sill, and Louis grabbing hold of William's paw, pulled him through the window and they both landed on the pavement outside and slunk down the drain into another world.

Chapter 7

William and Monsieur Louis go Time Travelling.

At least it was another world for William. William had thought when they left home that it was night time, but in fact as they emerged from the drain pipe over the other side of Fontevraud, it was the most beautiful of sunshiny days with a clear blue sky and fluffy clouds.

They had a fine time visiting a local château that William was convinced was in fact a castle just for cats as there seemed to more cats than humans that day. There were big cats, medium sized cats, small cats and some really tiny cats.

"Goodness", said William "I've never seen cats that small before".

"Oh it's them again" said Louis somewhat disdainfully. "In fact they are not locals at all but are on a day trip from Mars or some such planet. I'm not quite sure where they are from, but they tend to appear most places that I visit. They are known as the Teeny Weenies and wherever they go they make the most frightful noise".

Teenie weenies screaming through the universe

They might be "teeny weenie" but I can tell you now that they are usually very loud and can be quite boisterous", added Louis.

William put his nose in the air, swished his tail and moved on. The next he knew Louis had whisked him away up to one of the galleried rooms in the château where a number of cats were dancing to some rather old fashioned music. There was also a small orchestra at the side of the gallery all dressed in black and white.

"What strange clothes they are wearing. What year is this?"

"It's 1867 and these cats are dancing a new dance from Austria called a Waltz".

William asked if they might dance too.

"Well, Monsieur William we could do" said Louis, but I think that we should wait until we are asked don't you? In fact although it looks easy enough, the waltz is quite a complicated dance, so we should try to learn it before we start strutting about on the dance floor?"

William agreed that Louis was probably right and that any dancing would be better left for another day.

"Also it's very hot in here, wouldn't you rather go and sit in the shade somewhere and have a cool drink and a snooze?"

"Not really" said William explaining that he was much too excited to sleep.

"Not even a cat-nap?" Louis enquired.

"Not even that" said William.

And so the friends spent the day touring the château. They looked at everything including some really ancient furniture and richly coloured tapestries, that looked like carpets, but that hung on the walls. One of them was of a beautiful white horse with a golden horn on its forehead.

"What an unusual looking horse Louis".

"Oh him", said Louis "he is no ordinary horse. He is a unicorn who, so the legend goes, has many magical powers, though I am not convinced of it.

The last time I saw one he was getting up to all sorts of mischief popping out from behind trees and making people jump and walking about with a strange lady in a big hat and frightening us cats *and* children". He went on...."All sorts of people go looking for the unicorn and crowd up the forests. It can be such a nuisance".

"Why do they do that?" asked William".

"Well, they believe that if they find him they will also find wealth, happiness and love and such like nonsense. I personally think that he is overrated and just enjoys trooping about looking beautiful and causing havoc".

William looked disappointed so Louis reassured him saying

"Maybe one day we will go looking for him in the forests around Fontevraud l'abbaye where he has been known to pop up from time to time".

"Have *you* actually seen him Louis"?" William asked.

Louis said that although he didn't visit the forest that often, on the few times that he had, he had glimpsed the unicorn on one or two of his visits coaxing walkers off the paths and leading them astray and into the depths of the forest until they were lost.

Louis went on "People believe that to touch a unicorn's golden horn will bring them good luck and possibly even treasure"

"What fun it would be to find the unicorn", declared William. "That is if the legend is true".

"Of course the story is true in so far as people have for centuries believed it to be so" replied Louis., "though whether touching the unicorn will bring you treasure is another matter".

"It probably does account for the fact of why the unicorn likes to have some fun of his own with those who are trying to touch or even capture him", explained Louis..and is why he is forever trying to elude them and lead them astray".

"Well" said William, "my family could certainly do with some wealth, though he felt that his parents were okay on the love and happiness front. After all they did have him to love...

"Well, don't get too excited. We might not find him, and if we do there is no saying that it will bring us any wealth."

William was excited anyway to think that a unicorn might be living in the forest at the back of his house.

Then a very strange thing happened. William began to feel most peculiar.

First he quivered, and began to wobble. Then he felt as if he was melting into the tapestry.

Next thing that he knew he was in the depths of the forest of Fontevraud on the hillside looking down at the village and his house. How extraordinary thought William.

Suddenly William heard a movement by a holly tree and was a little frightened as emerging from behind the tree he saw a magnificent white horse with a beautiful silvery white mane and a golden horn that glistened in the sunlight. William could also see that unlike the unicorn in the picture that he had seen, this one seemed to have wings.

"Are you the unicorn?" asked William". And to his surprise the unicorn replied "Some call me by that name, but who are you?"

*Just the touching the horn of a unicorn may bring
you good luck*

"My name is William and I live down there in the village of Fontevraud". William pointed with his paw. "And if you look closely you can even see my house from up here in the forest".

"What are **you** doing in the forest today?" asked the Unicorn.

"Well", replied William, "strangely enough I didn't really plan to come. I was simply looking at a picture of you and no sooner had I thought that it would be rather nice to meet you then "wham" I found myself here!".

"Then you must be a very special cat William, because not many get the chance to see me, let alone talk to me. Why did you want to see me?"

"Because I was told by my dear friend Louis that you could bring all sorts of nice things to whomsoever see you. Is that true?"

"Nice things come in many forms, could you be a bit more specific? replied the unicorn.

"I don't want to appear greedy, but I had heard that whoever gets to touch your golden horn will receive great riches".

"It doesn't quite work like that", he explained, but what I can promise you is that I will always be your friend, and if you are ever in serious trouble I will help you if I possibly can".

Next the unicorn asked if William wanted to ride on his back.

"Oh yes please", replied William "is that why you have wings, so that you can fly?"

No sooner had William uttered these words then the unicorn unfurled his huge white wings and William found himself flying across the forest and village of Fontevraud.

"I didn't realise that Unicorns had wings", said William bemused.

"Well", said the Unicorn, "I am quite different from any other unicorn that you may know so that probably accounts for it".

"Well actually you are the first Unicorn that I have ever met, but how come you are so different and how come you have wings?" asked William. William was intrigued.

"My Grandfather was a Pegasus, and my Mother and Father were Unicorns", explained the Unicorn, "So that is why".

Looking down from a great height on the back of his new friend, William and the Unicorn "whooshed" through the air. William could see the abbey and St. Michel's church and the shops, along with cats, dogs and people all looking a little bit flat as he was so high up.

"Wheee...." William cried out..."This is the most exciting time of my life!"

"Let us follow the path of the Loire River", called out the Unicorn.

With the wind in his fur and riding majestically on the back of the unicorn William felt like a prince. Actually his parents had named him after the English Prince William and he now felt for the first time in his life, truly regal.

The two flew across the many lush green fields and vineyards, over towns and cities and of course the winding splendour of the Loire River.

"I can see my house", declared William. "Thank you so much for showing me all of this. I guess this is what they mean when they say that a view is panoramic!"

"Well it is quite nice for me to have a companion as well", replied the Unicorn. "So often I am alone and I don't fly as much as I used to. People want to meet me, but they don't really want friendship and adventure, they just want what they think I can do for them. I knew instantly that you William, would be a fun cat to be friends with".

William thanked the Unicorn very much. He felt very honoured that in the space of days he had made friends not only with a French cat in the form of Monsieur Louis, but also made friends with the mythical Unicorn who had given him this wonderful adventure.

Gradually the Unicorn and William settled to the ground and were back in the forest again.

"Now I think that you should leave as I think that there is going to be a storm".

William suddenly remembered the Unicorn's promise that he would help him if ever he were in trouble.

"How will you know if I am in trouble?" William enquired.

The unicorn replied that he could usually tell if any of his friends were in any sort of trouble and was used to coming to their rescue.

"You will know William, and so will I, as I will be able to feel any trouble you are in especially if you contact me".

"Of course", he went on. "You could always call out the magic words and then I would be bound to hear them wherever you are".

"Oh yes, that might help. What are they though?" asked William.

"Abracadabra of course! Really, for such an intelligent cat you can sometimes be quite silly".

William apologised profusely.

"You must say the word three times or it won't work. I am also going to give you a present of this silver whistle for added protection, so that if I cannot quite hear the magic words then hopefully I will hear the whistle".

And with a neigh and a toss of his head the unicorn passed the silver whistle from between his teeth to William's paws. William attached the whistle to his collar.

"Thank you very much", said William "I will keep it safe always".

Then no sooner had he appeared than the unicorn shook his lovely mane and vanished. William began to run down the slopes of the forest as the winds were beginning to pick up and he could hear the terrible wailing sound of the North wind. He ran and ran until he fell over and began to roll like a big fluffy ball down the hillside.

"Ouch! Ouch!" cried out William as he rolled right through the forest and landed upside down back at the château and found himself staring up into the eyes of a puzzled Louis.

"Wherever, have you been? asked his very concerned friend. "I thought that you had been abducted by the creatures from Mars. You look a complete mess!"
.
"Well I've not been abducted by aliens, no nothing like that, I was just staring at the tapestry of the unicorn thinking how nice it would be to meet him, when I came over all strange and I think that I was sucked into the picture".

"Sucked into it. Are you sure?"

The fact that William was covered in bits of old twig and bracken seemed to point to the truth of the matter.

 At the very least it was proof that he had recently been tumbling about in a forest and not just walking sedately around a château.

"Well", said Louis. "This just goes to show how if you think about things too much then all sorts of things can happen".

"I suppose so Louis, but although I am a bit bruised I really am quite glad that I met the unicorn as he was very friendly and said that if I ever got into trouble he would try to help me".

Chapter 8

The two friends continued their tour of the château. Next they came across some beautiful paintings on an oak panelled wall. William found himself staring wide-eyed at one of them.

"That is one of my relatives" Louis informed William as he stared up at a rather pretty cat dressed in pink with a parasol. Which for those of you who do not know is a kind of umbrella that some cats use to shield their faces from catching too much sun.

"She is an ancestor of mine called, Lady Henrietta Catkett (also known as Hetty). She is from the Eighteenth century".

William thought that she had the prettiest of faces and wondered if they were to travel even further back in the past whether in fact he might meet her.

"Quite possibly, Mon Ami", said Louis. William felt happy. He was happy because it was good to have the kind of friend who not only called you "friend", but now it seemed that he would be happy to introduce him to members of his family. William felt honoured.

William suddenly wondered why everyone in the past seemed to be a cat.

And as if Louis could ready William's mind he replied.

"Well because we are cats we tend to relate to our cat ancestors when we travel back in time. If we want to visit people from the past we need to put in a special request to the King of Magic, Merlin, but it is quite an involved process, and quite frankly more trouble then it is worth".

"How do we make contact with the King of Magic then?" William enquired.

"You can try writing to him and posting the letter down the drain or failing that you can wish very very hard. Sometimes he responds", replied Louis.

William agreed that it did seem rather a lot of effort and actually he did find writing rather difficult though sometimes his human parents did try to help him".

"Save it for another day William I think".

William agreed and they continued to watch the rather elegant dancing in front of them. Soon the dance was over and their visit completed. Night was falling and it was time to leave. The clock at the château struck dawn, but no sooner had they got outside of the château gates than they saw two cats having a sword fight.

"Good gracious", said William, "should they be doing that?"

Louis explained that they should not really be doing it as they were clearly having a duel and that duelling was now against the law.

"Tell them to stop, tell them to stop" said William who was feeling rather frightened lest they get tired of fighting each other and turn their swords on the two friends.

Suddenly two Gendarmes arrived and the men were arrested. Then just as some more Gendarmes seemed about to turn their attention in Louis and William's direction Louis called out

"Time for us to go I think".

The two slid down the nearest drain that they could find and were back in Fontevraud in no time. Once home again they said their goodbyes and Louis promised to call again the very next night. William again literally collapsed into his cat-basket and slept all day long with the images from his visit to the castle washing over him in his dreams.

Chapter 9

William awoke sixteen hours later feeling terribly hungry, so he raced down to his cat bowls and gobbled down one whole bowl of delicious cat-food. Just as he finished his meal to his surprise he could hear voices coming from the Dining Room. Are my parents home he wondered? He pushed open the Dining-Room door and to his astonishment he could quite clearly see that Monsieur Louis was seated in the best chair (the one with the tall, carved back and the golden upholstery that he loved to scratch).

Louis was entertaining none other than the pretty cat, he had seen in the painting at the castle, Lady Henrietta Catkett. They were drinking creamy coffees and eating croissants.

"Bonjour, Monsieur William", said Louis gesturing for William to sit down "do come and join us". William now knew that bonjour in French meant "good-day, but he was not at all convinced that it was a good day as he was a little put out by what he saw as an intrusion. Of course he liked Louis very much, but the very idea of just barging into his home was rather upsetting.

"Do accept my apologies. We did knock, but again you were fast asleep so I thought it best if we waited for you to wake up.

Hetty is only here for a few hours as she's on her way to the future and thought that she would drop in to see me and perhaps also visit the abbey. Of course I knew that you wanted to meet her, so I invited her up for a coffee. Hope you don't mind. Would you like one?

William suddenly felt very shy, as Hetty was indeed a lovely cat with silver-grey fur, almond shaped eyes and very long whiskers, which were covered in cream.

William was flabbergasted at the audacity of his new found friend. William also thought Hetty a very pretty little cat. So pretty in fact that he forgave Louis for barging into his home uninvited and unannounced.

"No coffee for me", said William in a squeaky voice. He cleared his throat, "but I am very pleased to meet you Lady Henrietta".

"Enchanté Monsieur William", she replied which Louis explained meant that she was pleased to meet him too.

"Oh, and do call me Hetty", she replied.

William suddenly had an idea.

"I know, let's go to the abbey together. You see I've never been, but I'd love to go.

Then perhaps you could both "sleep over" here and then we could all go on to the future".

They all agreed that it was a splendid idea to visit the abbey that day. Louis wasn't quite sure if William was quite up to visiting the future yet as "it is a very hectic place".

"We might have to leave that until you are a more experienced traveller", said Louis. "Anyway", he went on, "there is no need to time travel this time...let's just walk along the street in the present".

Chapter 10

The three cats then jumped through the window onto the pavement outside William's house and trooped in single file next door to Fontevraud Abbey. As they arrived a group of school children were walking through the large courtyard. William saw Melody and ran up to her and wove himself in and out of her legs purring richly.

"Bonjour Le Chat. Ca va?" said Melody which of course meant that she wished him a good day and wondered how he was?

"Very well, thank you", William surprised himself as for the first time he found himself meowing in French..."Ca va bien, merci".

William felt extremely pleased with himself, or as his Mother would have put it had she been there; "as pleased as punch" whatever that was supposed to mean.

William introduced Melody to Louis and to "Lady Henrietta Catkett". Melody looked amazed to be meeting an aristocrat.

"You can call me Hetty", she told Melody.

Melody asked if the three cats would like to come round the abbey with her and her chums.

They all agreed that this would be a fun thing to do.

Chapter 11

William discovered that there is nothing nicer than sightseeing with a group of really friendly cats and children. Together they looked at the ancient tombs of the Angevin Kings and Queens, the huge vaults of the abbey and the old Romanesque Kitchens that are round and according to Melody

"The only example of this kind of building left in the world".

Everyone was impressed by Melody's knowledge as she had done her homework. William could almost smell the fragrant cooking smells from the past. He thought that he could see the remnants of an old spit where many years ago, meat would have been roasted over a fire, but Louis told him that he was imagining things.

Next it was out into the grounds of the abbey and because it was the height of summer, the gardens really were filled with the gorgeous smells of honeysuckle, roses and various blossoms and grasses. Scampering about the undergrowth were cats and rats, and even toads. William felt as if he was back again in England as he chased a little brown field mouse. The little mouse, who was petrified, turned round and cried out "Oh please don't eat me".

"Only playing", teased William in reply and the field mouse scampered off. Now he no longer had the problem of mice back at home, he was beginning to feel quite fond of them again.

"I will chase them", said William, "but I will not hurt them".

William was overjoyed to be roaming free around the grounds of the abbey when suddenly he fell over a small golden box and landed on the other side of it.

William, feeling a little dizzy, stared at it for quite a long time as it was a most remarkable looking box encrusted with jewels of many colours of topaz orange, rose quartz and amethyst mauve.

Just as William was about to lift the lid of the strange box Louis came up behind him and whispered

"Be careful what you do", he cautioned. "This is a very special golden casket filled with memories, that if you unleash them you must be prepared to face any consequences. There might be for example some bad memories, even nightmares trapped in there. Of course there might be some wonderful memories.

You just have to be aware that there are a number of possible outcomes to you opening it".

Louis told William that the casket had belonged to Richard the Lionheart who had brought it back from Constantinople in Turkey when he was on one of his crusades in the Twelfth Century.

"What are crusades and where is Constantinople?" asked William I've never heard of either".

"Well, said Louis, you do ask a lot of questions and it's a long story, but basically crusaders were men who wanted to bring the Holy Lands mentioned in the Bible into their power in the name of their religion. Anyone who was not a Christian they labelled as a heathen. This caused no end of problems which still have repercussions today".

William found it all rather complicated, but he thought that Constantinople sounded a very interesting place. And as if Louis could read William's thoughts he suddenly said, "Oh, and Constantinople is now called Istanbul which is indeed a very interesting and special place full of ancient treasures and magnificent buildings".

"Like the abbey?" enquired William.

Louis explained that some of them were covered in gold and other precious materials and that many centuries ago the abbey would undoubtedly have had richly coloured frescos on its walls and that if you look at some of the walls you can still see, though they are now faded, some of the wonderful paintings.

"Is there no way of telling if there is a good memory that we can unleash? Couldn't I just have a little peek?" asked William. "I don't feel a bit scared".

"No William, not even just a little peek, as I could not account for what dreadful things might happen".
Louis was distracted by a call from Melody and her friends who wanted to play with a little rubber ball. As Louis was a retriever cat and loved to run after anything that was thrown in the air, especially little rubber balls which he would bound after and bring back to whosoever had thrown it, he rushed across. Hetty had already begun to play.

"Are you coming William?"

"In a minute Louis", he replied.

William was in a particularly naughty mood that day and really wanted to find out what memories might be in the casket. He cautiously lifted the lid and some small green creatures with wings and little cat faces, flew out and round William's head making the most alarming screeching sound. William was absolutely terrified.

"Louis, Louis save me, save me".

Louis and also Hetty came running over to rescue William.

"Are you alright William", asked a very worried Hetty.

"I'm scared Hetty...look out" and as William spoke the little cat dragons swooped around the heads of the three friends.

"Can you stop them Louis"?"

"Well I'm not really sure that I can or even should as I told you *not* to open the casket".
William felt so ashamed.

"I'm so sorry Louis I just couldn't resist".

Louis suggested that they duck down and hide under a tree" and the three cats crouched under an ancient plum tree.

"Oh dear", said William "What on earth shall we do?"

"Well it might be too late now as you have unleashed the cat dragons and there is no saying what will happen...I shall try one thing and hope and pray that it works!"

"Cat dragons, what are they?" William shrieked, as yet again the little beasts flew around his head.

"I'll tell you later on William – if there is a later on that is".

Louis tried to shoo the cat dragons back into the casket by running up close to it and jumping quickly out of the way just as the cat dragons landed. Hetty also tried to help. But no matter how hard they tried they could not coax the little monsters back into the casket.

In fact the more they tried the more screeching sounds the dragons made, and as they cackled and cawed the skies began to get dark and the air was freezing cold.

What horror is this? The little cat dragons attack!

"As they cackled and cawed the skies began to get dark and the air froze".

The grounds of the abbey had become a very frightening place.

"Oh it's hopeless, it hasn't worked, they just won't go back in", cried out Louis and Hetty together. The two ran back to William who was still hiding under the old plum tree.

Then suddenly William remembered the Unicorn and how he had said that if ever he were in trouble he would try to help him. William called out the magic words.

"Abracadabra, Abracadabra" William cried out "Oh dear I can't remember if the unicorn said say the word two or three times. How silly of me".

"Try to remember William, try to remember". Hetty remonstrated with him.

William cried out one more Abracadabra, but still nothing happened and the cat dragons were flying all around the plum tree and the day was getting darker and darker, colder and colder. There was lightening and thunder, hailstones and snow all at the same time.

Then William remembered the little silver whistle that the unicorn had given him. He detached it from his collar and blew it sharply.

"I'm not sure whether or not this will work, but let's hope so".

Then a very strange thing happened the rain, sleet and snow stopped and so did the thunder. The skies began to change and instead of being grey and black and freezing they were flooded with shimmering lights of rose and gold threaded with sliver streams of light that pointed like enormous fingers down to the grounds of the abbey. Suddenly the unicorn appeared flying down one of the streams and landed right next to the old plum tree.

Then as quickly as the little green cat dragons had appeared, they flew back screeching all the way back into the golden casket.

William looked out to the unicorn and smiled

"Thank you, you have saved us from the green monsters".

"Any time", replied the Unicorn. "It is a pleasure to help you and your friends. I must return now back to the forests. Farewell".

"Au revoir Monsieur Unicorn", all three cats called out in harmony.

"Take care", said William. "We hope to see you again, but not just if we are in trouble".

"No indeed", replied the Unicorn. "Well, I will be in touch as they say. Perhaps William you and your friends would like a journey across the skies?"

"Oh yes please", William replied enthusiastically, that would be terrific!"

They all agreed that this would be splendid as they waved goodbye to the Unicorn who flew back into the golden clouds.

"Well that wasn't *so* bad was it and at least those cat dragons have gone", said Louis?"

"Oh Louis, not so bad! Apart from meeting the Unicorn again, I was terrified.

"Well, it serves you right, I did tell you not to open the casket", Louis reprimanded William, "Perhaps next time you will listen to what I say".

Chapter 12

William again apologised and said how sorry he was to have opened the casket. He promised never do anything like that again.

"I kept thinking that it couldn't really hurt, and that I might get a lovely memory instead of those little monsters. What on earth were those horrible things?"

Louis explained that they were little cat-dragons from the middle- ages when there were many dragons which breathed fire and caused a lot of havoc wherever they went.

"Long ago when there were Knights in shining armour and ladies in distress, Knights would go out of their way to save them from the dragons. One particular Knight was called George and people of that time were so impressed by how brave he was that they made him a Saint".

"Oh I've heard of him in England. We have a Saints Day called "St. Georges. Is that the same George?"

Louis confirmed that it was and that in fact this George was also born in the Middle East so wasn't actually English at all.

The story goes that George was adopted as the patron saint of soldiers after he apparently appeared to the Crusader army at the Battle of Antioch in 1098 during the first crusades.

"Not English then", William replied. "History seems to be terribly mixed up doesn't it. I am really quite confused and tired".

"Me too William" said Hetty.

"I think then," that is quite enough of an adventure for us today, shall we go home?"

"Oh yes please Louis." William was suddenly feeling very tired indeed. "Would you like to spend the night at my house?"

"Not today William, though maybe another time".

Hetty also explained that she had to get to an outer space party "but " she added "I would simply love to visit you again in the future." With these words she left, but not without giving William a really squashy kiss.

Lady Henrietta Catkett
Pretty in pink..

"Mon Chéri, it has been *so adorable* to meet you" and with a flash of her rather glamorous stole and diamond eyes, she was gone.

Although William was sad that Hetty, and also Louis, had left he was equally relieved as the idea of entertaining two guests to dinner along with entertainments which they were sure to want, was something he was too tired to face.

And so they said their good byes to Melody and her friends and left the abbey.

Chapter 13

Where William falls asleep and discovers that it may all have been a dream....

William awoke to the sound of his parents banging in their usual fashion. He rushed down from the attic and looked down the various landings of the banisters his little face peering down each stairwell of the banister.

"Meow, Meow", cried William. Which his parents knew meant that he was asking where had they been?

William's parents looked at him lovingly and kissed and hugged him as they usually did when he woke up in the morning.

"Oh isn't he sweeeeeet..." said Mother.

"Been William", added Father. "We've been to bed, but that's about as exciting as it gets..."

William was beginning to feel quite paranoid as it suddenly occurred to him that in fact if his parents had not been away, there may well have been no adventures with cats at all let alone a beautiful unicorn and little pesky cat dragons.

Has it all been just a dream questioned William and meowed out in distress to his parents.

"Poor wee thing, you must be coming down with a cold", said Mother.

Then she gave him an extra squeeze, which William hated, and a kiss, which he loved.

William began to cry.

"Oh dear, sweet William, what on *earth* is the matter?" his parents called out together.

William's parents had only soothing words and love to give to William and settled him into bed and read stories to him including nearly the whole of Sleeping Beauty before he fell into a deep, deep sleep.

Chapter 14

William awoke to the sound of the church bells tolling the hour of eight o' clock in the morning. It was a bright and sunny day and William wondered what the day held in store for him.

He suddenly remembered that none of the exciting things that he thought had happened had really happened which was terribly confusing. And still there was that wretched road to cross from his house.

William looked across the road and saw a sunny and dusty step that looked inviting to him and strangely familiar.

"Go on William, do go out", said Mother. "I am sure that it will be fun if you do", she added reassuringly.

And so William darted across the road, after looking very carefully that is from left to right. He sniffed the step and settled down to watch his house and the characters who walked past as he sat.

Just as he was beginning to fall into a siesta (he had had a big breakfast) he heard the familiar sound of a cat calling the following words:

"Hey you, Monsieur…what do you think you are doing on *my* doorstep?" Next the cat said the following words…

"I'm only joking William. "Why are you looking at me as if you didn't know me? Come on move over and make room for me!"

William moved over to let Louis sit down. He suddenly came to the conclusion that not only had he not been dreaming about all the adventures that he had had, but that Louis was really his friend and that also he understood his French meows perfectly.

William also realised that although he may have dreamt the note from his parents informing him that they had gone away, everything else had been real. He was both relieved and elated.

Then Melody, on her way to school, stopped and patted them both on their heads.

"Au revoir mes chéris, à bientôt", she called out as she moved on. Which of course means goodbye my darlings see you later.

William suddenly knew that he was going to be very happy in his new home, in this new country. And what is more he felt sure that he would soon be going on lots more exciting adventures with his new friends.

Entente Cordial – the best friends in the world

**William at the door at
Chez Teresa/A Taste d'Angleterre in
Fontevraud l'abbaye**

Teresa Dolan lives in Fontevraud in the Loire Valley in
the West of France next door to the twelfth century abbey
where Eleanor of Aquitaine and her son, Richard the
Lionheart are buried. She is married to Tony, has a son
called Jay , a cat called William, and a new addition to
the family is Mini, a wild cat who recently refused to
leave the family doorstep. Together they all run a Salon
de Thé/petite restaurant and Chambres d'hôtes in this
ancient and beautiful village and have done so since
2006.

Check out their blog at and websites on

www.lettersandlunchesfromtheloire.com

& wwwchezteresa.com.

A book featuring popular treats from their tea room called Chez Teresa: Sweets and Treats is available on Amazon.

Teresa finds the Loire Valley generally a rich source of inspiration for her writing. She plans to develop more stories in the future. *The Fontevraud Cat* is the first book in a planned series about a time-travelling cat called William. Teresa is also currently in the process of developing a series of short stories featuring her god-child and niece Alisha-Joy. Alisha Joy and the Blue Fairy is available now. Also in the pipeline is a short story for the Rosie May Foundation.

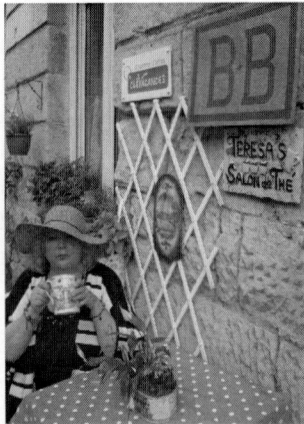